Daddy's Promise

Daddy's Promise

by

Cindy Klein Cohen

John T. Heiney

Illustrations by

Michael J. Gordon

Promise Publications

Bloomfield Hills, Michigan

Published in the United States of America

by

Promise Publications

6632 Telegraph Rd., #117

Bloomfield Hills, MI   48301

e-mail address: promisepubs@juno.com

ISBN: 0-9656498-0-6

BJ

Library of Congress Catalog Card Number: 96-93084

First Edition April, 1997

Second Edition April, 2003

AUTHORS' NOTE

Our story is about a little boy's journey of discovery after the death of his father. Jesse is angry and filled with questions. Why did his daddy have to die? What happens when someone dies? Where do they go? Jesse's questions are answered by both his mother and a series of dreams where Jesse visits his father and learns about life, death and life after death.

Through Jesse's mother, the book answers common questions children have about death, as well as suggestions for coping. Concrete, simple explanations are given for what happens when someone dies. During dream-like visits with his father, Jesse learns more about death, what happens when we die and where our spirits go.

Through his open interactions with his mother and father, Jesse is able to find positive messages. He finds that death is not an ending; it is the beginning of a new existence. He learns the answers to his questions: Where does the soul/spirit go when someone dies? What happens in the special place? What role does the soul/spirit play in the lives of loved ones on Earth? Most importantly, Jesse learns that his daddy will always be watching over him, to guide him throughout his life.

In all cases, Jesse's questions are answered honestly and are treated with respect, care and compassion. Our hope is that this book will help open a healthy dialogue between adults and children where loss has occurred, where the mystery and fear of death can be replaced with comfort and hope.

On a personal note, Cindy's husband died in 1992, when her son was almost two years old. Since that time, he has related many dreams and "encounters" with his father, in addition to the expected questions. These experiences, along with professional knowledge and spiritual "intuition," led to the creation of this book.

CKC

JTH

ACKNOWLEDGEMENTS

The authors' heartfelt thanks to everyone who helped us along the journey to publish this book, especially Pat Bagchi; Sharon Baseman; Micki and John Baumann; Ronnie and Barbara Cohen; Sonya Friedman, Ph.D.; Don and Eileen Klein; Deanne Ginns-Gruenberg, MA, LLP, LPC, BSN; Barry Jay, Ph.D.; Wayne Johnson; Bob Michael; Robert Shook; and Alicia Tisdale, Ph.D. Thanks also to our family and friends for their support and encouragement. Thanks to Borders Books and Music for providing the environment and the coffee to help our creativity flow. Finally . . . to all the publishers who turned us down for empowering us to do this our way!

Michael J. Gordon would like to acknowledge Sharon Baseman, without whom none of this would be possible; his father — no matter what age you are, when your father dies, you're still his little boy; his mother, who teaches us that life continues even when you wish it wouldn't, but it's okay; and Eric, you know why.

DEDICATIONS

For Joe, alav ha'shalom, and Alec
— the inspirations for this book.

CKC

To Alice, Paige and Clark. For
Lillian — may you find love and
light on your journey.

JTH

To Robert, the brother I never
knew, but I know is always with
me.

MJG

It was a bright, warm, beautiful spring day. The neighborhood was buzzing with activity. People were out walking, working on their lawns, playing baseball in the park. It was the kind of day Jesse had wished for all winter long.

Jesse was not outside on this warm day. He really didn't feel like being outside. He was looking for a baseball mitt. The mitt his Daddy had promised him last fall, on a warm day just like this.

Jesse remembered that day.

He and his Daddy were playing catch. Daddy had promised him that in the spring, as soon as baseball season started, he would give him a special mitt. The mitt that had been his own as a child. "You're not quite big enough for it now," Daddy said. "But in the spring, it will fit you perfectly, and I'll be there to watch you play."

But things didn't work out that way. Jesse's Daddy got very sick. As the weather grew colder, his Daddy grew worse.

The doctors told Mommy they were doing all they could, but the medicines they were using weren't working. One day, just before spring arrived, Daddy's body stopped working, and he died.

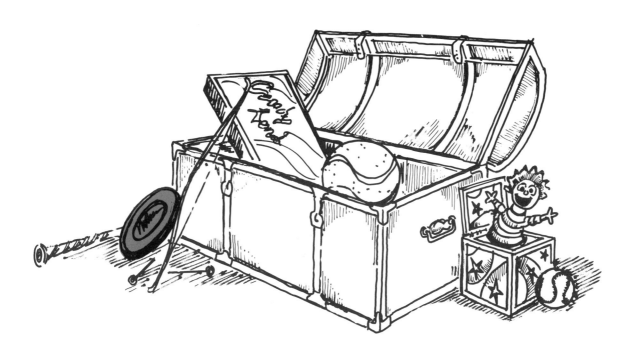

Jesse thought about his Daddy as he looked for the mitt. He looked everywhere. He tore his room apart, hoping his Daddy had left it for him somewhere, but he couldn't find it. Finally, he stopped looking and started to cry.

Jesse's Mommy walked by and saw him crying.

She asked, "What's wrong, Jesse?"

"I can't find my baseball mitt," he said. "I didn't want to play that dumb game anyway."

"But, honey, you were so excited to play. Your league starts next week. Besides, I know Daddy would be so proud to watch you. He would want you to play."

"He said he would give me his special mitt, but he didn't," Jesse said angrily.

"Jesse, I'm sure Daddy wanted you to have the mitt," Mommy said. "I'm sure he put it away for you. I'll go through his things. I promise I'll look for it."

"But Daddy said he would be here to watch me, and now he's gone," Jesse cried. "He lied to me."

"Jesse, Daddy didn't lie to you. He didn't know he would die. He wanted to be here more than anything."

"Why did Daddy have to die?" Jesse asked. "Did I do something wrong?"

"Nothing you did or said made Daddy die. It wasn't your fault. It wasn't anyone's fault. We don't know why it happened. It just happened."

"Why did he leave me? He knew I was supposed to play. Why did he die?"

"Jesse, Daddy didn't choose to die."

"But I want to see him," Jesse said.

"I know, Jesse, but we can't. Daddy's not coming back. When someone dies we can't see them or touch them anymore, but we can remember and love them. We can look at Daddy's pictures and videos."

"But where did he go?"

"Remember at the cemetery, we put Daddy's body in the ground," Mommy said. "His body stopped working, and we needed a place to put it. That's what cemeteries are for.

"They put Daddy's body in the ground, but not Daddy," she said. "What we remember and love about Daddy will always be with us, here and here." With that, Mommy touched her head and her heart.

"We can remember him with pictures, thoughts and in our memories.

"The person you remember as Daddy was his spirit. That will live on. That's what we will remember whenever we think of him."

That night, when Jesse went to bed he thought about what Mommy said. "Daddy's spirit lives on. . ."

As he drifted off to sleep, he looked out at the stars and thought. "I wonder if my Daddy's out there."

That night, Jesse had a wonderful dream. He dreamed he was walking up a hill carrying an orange balloon. He walked all the way to the top of the hill. When he reached the top, the balloon lifted him up and he floated gently to the sky. He went up and up, through the clouds and into the heavens.

He looked around. He felt like he was floating in a big, bright cloud. There were lights all around him. He felt safe and warm, and, most of all, he felt loved.

At that moment, Jesse floated up to his Daddy's arms. "Hi, Daddy," he said. "Daddy, I miss you so much, but where are we? What is this place?"

"We are in a very special place," Daddy said. "This is where we go when our bodies stop working and our spirits are ready to leave the Earth."

"But Mommy said I wouldn't be able to see you anymore and that you wouldn't be able to hug me anymore."

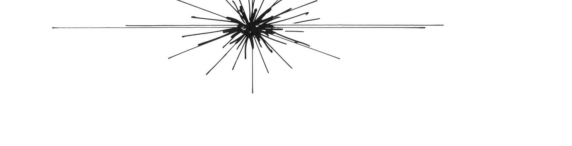

"Mommy's right, not like you used to on Earth. But because you think of me, love me and remember me, I am able to be with you in this way right now."

"Mommy said your body stopped working. That's why you died," Jesse said. "Did it hurt when you died?"

"No," Daddy said. "When your body stops working, you don't feel any pain."

"But why are you here?"

"Remember, Jesse, this is where we come when our bodies stop working. My body stopped working, but my spirit lives on. This is the place where my spirit came when I died."

"Who do you live with here? Are you alone?"

"Oh, no, there are lots of other people here, even some people you know," Daddy said. "Remember when Zachary's grandpa died?"

Jesse remembered. Zachary had been very sad.

"Well, he's here and he's doing fine," Daddy said. "He watches over Zachary every day."

"What do you do here?"

"Everybody does different things," Daddy said. "Mostly, we come here to think about what we've learned and where we'll go next. I've chosen to stay here and watch over you and Mommy."

"But if you can choose," said Jesse, "why don't you choose to come home and be with us?"

"That's not a choice I can make," Daddy said. "I am with you, but in *this* way. I am with you here and here." Daddy touched his heart and his head.

Jesse remembered when his Mommy said the same thing.

"That's what Mommy said, too," he said.

"Can I stay here with you? I promise I'll be good."

"I want to be with you more than anything," said Daddy. "But it's not about you being good. It's not your time to be here now. You have to go back and be with Mommy."

"But why can't Mommy come too?"

"It's not her time to be here either," Daddy said gently. "You both have much more to learn and do on Earth. Besides, I need a favor that only you can do for me. I need you to go back and tell Mommy that I'm OK and that this is a good place."

Jesse promised his Daddy he would deliver his message, and then he gave him a big, wonderful hug. And with that, Daddy floated him gently, like a feather, back down through the heavens and into his bed.

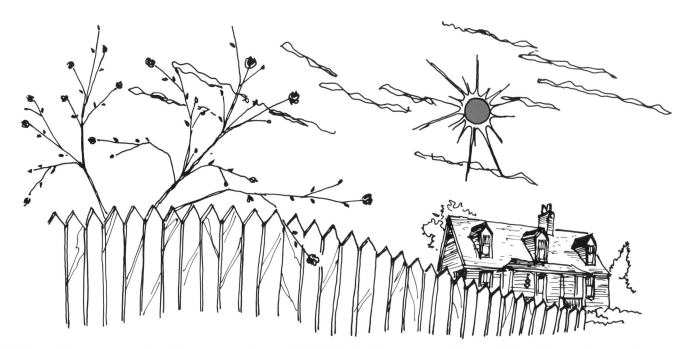

When Jesse awoke it was a beautiful, bright sunny day. The first thing he thought of was Daddy. He felt warm and safe, like he did when his Daddy hugged him.

Jesse was excited to share the news of his dream with Mommy.

Jesse told his Mommy all about his dream visit with Daddy. He told her about how Daddy was in a good place, a place where everyone goes when their body stops working.

Jesse told her that it didn't hurt when Daddy died. He told her that Daddy is not alone, and that he is with other people whose bodies stopped working.

"I wanted him to come home with me, but he couldn't," Jesse said. "He has to stay where he is and we have to stay where we are. He said *his* body stopped working, *ours* didn't.

"But Daddy said if we think of him, love him and remember him, he will be in our hearts and in our heads. Just like you said, Mommy."

Jesse's Mommy gave him a hug and said, "Do you feel better now that you saw Daddy in your dream?"

"Yes," Jesse answered. He did feel better. He felt safe and happy, knowing that his Mommy was with him and that his Daddy was watching over them.

Jesse was happy about his first visit with his Daddy, but still wondered why his Daddy had to leave the Earth. It just wasn't fair. Why did Daddy have to go? "I want him here," he thought.

That night, as he drifted off to sleep, he dreamed about the magic balloon. The balloon lifted him up and up, through the clouds and into the bright, beautiful heavens. A feeling of love surrounded him, and he knew his Daddy was near.

"I know you are still wondering why I had to leave you and Mommy," Daddy said. "There is no easy answer.

"I didn't choose to leave the earth, but it happened," Daddy said. "All things happen for a reason.

"Now that I am here, I understand that reason. I am here to watch over you and Mommy, and to teach you some very important things. I am here to help you and guide you through your life and the lessons you will learn."

"But what am I supposed to learn?" Jesse asked.

"Don't worry about that now," Daddy said. "As you get older, I will be there to guide you in your learning."

"Will I see you, like now?" Jesse asked.

"You may not always see me like you see me now, but know I will be there."

And with that, Daddy floated him gently, like a feather, back down through the heavens and into his bed.

Once again, when Jesse awoke the next morning, the first thing he thought of was his Daddy. He felt warm and safe. He ran downstairs to tell his Mommy about his second dream.

"Mommy," Jesse called. "I had another dream about Daddy."

Jesse told her all about his visit with Daddy. He told her that Daddy didn't choose to die, but now that he's there, he wants to watch over them.

"Daddy said there are a lot of things for me to learn and he's going to help me. All I have to do is think about him and he will be there to help. I won't always be able to see him, but he will be there. I wish Daddy was still here, but at least he can watch over us."

Jesse went to school that day with the same feeling he had when he was with his Daddy. He felt warm and safe. He had a very good day at school.

On his way home from school he walked past the baseball field. He saw his friends, and they asked him to play. Jesse wasn't ready to play. Without his Daddy watching, it just wouldn't be the same.

Then he thought about what his Daddy had said in his dream. He heard his Daddy's voice say, "Remember, you may not always be able to see me, but know that I am with you. I'll be watching over you."

Then Jesse said out loud, though no one could hear, "But I don't know where your mitt is. You promised I could have it."

Jesse walked on, remembering his Daddy's words, and wishing he could find the baseball mitt.

When Jesse came home, his Mommy was sitting in the kitchen.

He went in and sat down next to her.

"Have you thought any more about playing baseball?" she asked.

"Yea, a little," Jesse said, surprised that his Mommy was thinking about the same thing he was. "Why?"

"I was thinking about what you told me this morning," she said. "About what Daddy told you, that he would be there for you. You know, Daddy really wanted you to play baseball. I bet he would enjoy watching you."

"But I don't have his baseball mitt," Jesse said, a little frustrated.

And with that, Mommy reached over and pulled out the baseball mitt she had promised to look for.

"Would this help?" she smiled.

"Mommy, you found it! Where was it?" cried Jesse.

"I was going through some of Daddy's things and I found it tucked away in one of his drawers," she said with a tear in her eye. "He must have been keeping it there for you. See, it even has your name on it."

A note was attached. "For Jesse. Remember, I'll always be watching."

Jesse looked up to the heavens and realized his Daddy had heard his words. "Thank you, Daddy!" he said. "I understand now, you really are watching."

From that day on, Jesse knew that his Daddy would always be with him, watching him play baseball, watching him learn and grow. He knew that in this special way, his Daddy would be a part of him, for now and always.

ABOUT THE AUTHORS

Cindy Klein Cohen is a masters-prepared Child Life Specialist who has worked in a health care setting for over 10 years, helping children and their families cope with serious illness and loss. John Heiney holds a degree in communications and journalism, and has worked in health care for over eight years as a communications professional. Collaboratively they have created numerous resources and programs, both educational and therapeutic, for children. They have been published in a children's health care journal and have spoken at national conferences related to their work.

ABOUT THE ILLUSTRATOR

Michael J. Gordon graduated from The University of Michigan with a Bachelor of Science in Architecture and a Masters of Architecture. After having been employed by several Michigan architectural firms, he started his own practice in 1990, later to merge in 1992 to become Moiseev/Gordon Associates, Inc. Before undertaking the project of illustrating *Daddy's Promise*, Michael was noted for his scenic stage design, having helped mount many shows for St. Dunstan's of Cranbrook.

Photo by Bob Michael

PROMISE PUBLICATIONS
ORDER FORM

To order more copies of *Daddy's Promise*, complete this order form, cut at the dotted line, and send it with your check or money order payable to *Promise Publications,* along with your name, the name of your organization, if applicable, and your address, to:

Promise Publications

6632 Telegraph Road, #117

Bloomfield Hills, MI 48301

Phone: 248-865-9345   **E-mail address: promisepubs@juno.com**

Quantity	Price Each	Subtotal
_____ X	**$12.95**	$_____
	Sales Tax	_____
	If Michigan resident add 6 % of subtotal	
	Shipping	_____
	10% of subtotal (Minimum $3.50)	
	Total	$_____

For wholesale orders or more copies, call 248-865-9345 for terms and conditions.

If you would like to be added to our mailing list so we can let you know about additional products from Promise Publications, please fill in your name and address below:

Name: _____

Organization: _____

Street Address: _____

City, State, ZIP: _____

Phone Number: _____

E-mail Address: _____

PROMISE PUBLICATIONS
ORDER FORM

To order more copies of *Daddy's Promise*, complete this order form, cut at the dotted line, and send it with your check or money order payable to *Promise Publications,* along with your name, the name of your organization, if applicable, and your address, to:

Promise Publications
6632 Telegraph Road, #117
Bloomfield Hills, MI 48301

Phone: 248-865-9345   **E-mail address: promisepubs@juno.com**

Quantity		Price Each	Subtotal
_____	X	**$12.95**	$_____
		Sales Tax	_____
		If Michigan resident add 6 % of subtotal	
		Shipping	_____
		10% of subtotal (Minimum $3.50)	
		Total	$_____

For wholesale orders or more copies, call 248-865-9345 for terms and conditions.

If you would like to be added to our mailing list so we can let you know about additional products from Promise Publications, please fill in your name and address below:

Name:_____

Organization:_____

Street Address:_____

City, State, ZIP:_____

Phone Number:_____

E-mail Address:_____